HOW ANIMALS LIVE

First published in 1976
Usborne Publishing Ltd
20 Garrick Street
London WC2E 9BJ
© Usborne Publishing Ltd 1976

Published in Australia by
Rigby Limited
Adelaide, Sydney, Melbourne, Brisbane, Perth

Published in Canada by
Hayes Publishing Ltd, Burlington, Ontario

Printed in Belgium
by Henri Proost, Turnhout, Belgium.

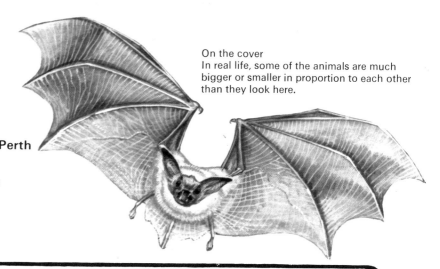

On the cover
In real life, some of the animals are much
bigger or smaller in proportion to each other
than they look here.

About This Book

This book is all about how animals live in the wild. It is full of exciting pictures and every page is packed with interesting and unusual facts about them—from the huge African elephant to the tiny vampire bat. It shows you how animals have their babies and how they look after them.

We show how animals live in different parts of the world—which ones sleep during the day and feed at night, how some stalk and kill their prey, and how some choose their mates.

You can read how polar bears teach their young to catch fish and how a camel survives in the desert without water. We answer such questions as 'How long can a hippo stay under-water?' 'How fast can a cheetah run?' and 'How do bats find their way in the dark?'

A map of the world on pages 44 and 45 shows all the different parts of the world where the animals live. On page 46 a special chart gives more than 300 easy-to-understand facts about their lives and habits.

HOW ANIMALS LIVE

Anne Civardi and Cathy Kilpatrick

Illustrated by George Thompson
Designed by Sally Burrough

Consultant: Michael Boorer
(Writer and Broadcaster)

CONTENTS

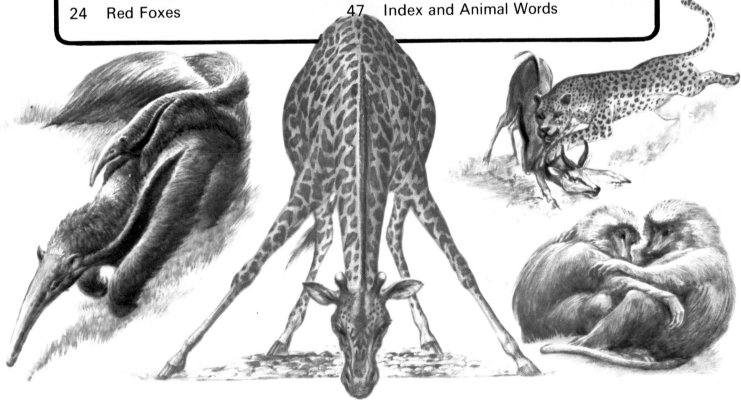

Chimpanzees and Other Apes

Chimpanzees are clever and are the animals most like people. They are a kind of ape. An ape is different from a monkey because it does not have a tail.

Chimps eat leaves, fruit and seeds. Sometimes they kill and eat small animals. Most of their day is spent on the ground cleaning each other and playing.

They use sticks and stones as tools to get food and to fight with. A big chimp might throw stones at an approaching enemy or hit it with a stick.

When chimps meet, they often hold hands, kiss and hug each other. If one is very upset or frightened, it runs to the other chimps for comfort. They touch and pat it to calm it down.

They talk to each other by making grunting and hooting noises. When they are very excited, chimpanzees bark loudly and jump up and down waving their arms in the air.

A mother chimpanzee takes great care of her baby. She feeds and cleans it and teaches it to do lots of different things. The baby suckles and sleeps close to her for at least four years.

Making Faces

This chimpanzee is thinking.

This one wants to play.

This chimp is hooting hello.

This one is very frightened.

Most grown-up chimps know that insects, called termites, make a delicious meal. This one has found a big termite mound and is poking a long stalk of grass down the holes to catch some.

After a while, he pulls the grass out and licks the insects off the end. Chimpanzees also use grass stalks and long, thin sticks to collect honey from bees' nests and to get ants out of ant-hills.

This chimp is sleeping high up in the tree top. Every night all chimps, except the babies, make nests of twigs and branches to sleep in. Sometimes they make pillows out of clumps of leaves.

Chimpanzees often get together to clean each other. They comb one another's hair with their fingers and pick off seeds, bits of dirt, scabs and ticks.

This baby chimpanzee is only a few months old. He rides about clinging to his mother's stomach. When he gets a bit older he will ride piggy-back.

Chimps usually walk and run on all fours. Sometimes they run downhill swinging their legs between their arms. They can go much faster like this.

Other Kinds of Apes

Gorillas are the biggest and strongest kind of ape. Usually they are quiet and shy, but if they get excited or angry they stand up and beat their chests.

This ape is called a siamang. He can fill a big sac under his chin with air to make a booming noise. When he lets the air out, he makes a loud shriek.

Gibbons are very acrobatic apes with extra-long arms and hooked fingers. They use them to swing between branches and to leap from tree to tree.

5

Giraffes

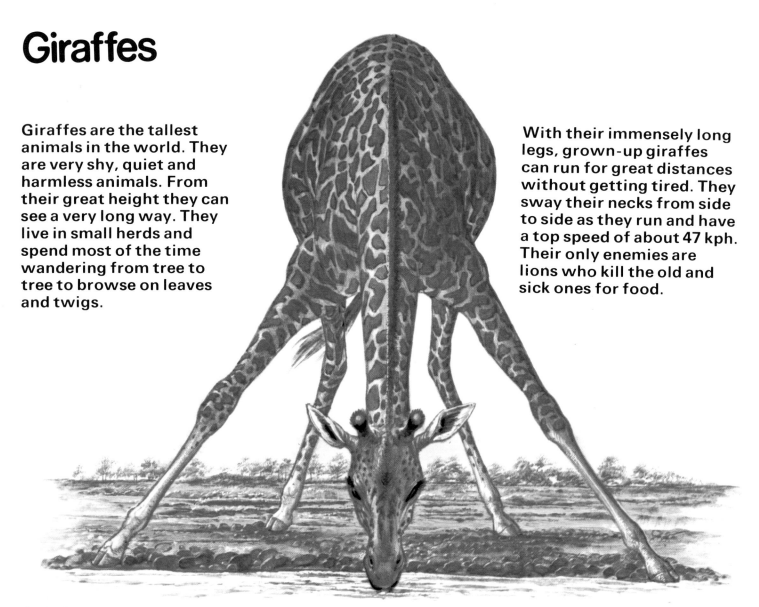

Giraffes are the tallest animals in the world. They are very shy, quiet and harmless animals. From their great height they can see a very long way. They live in small herds and spend most of the time wandering from tree to tree to browse on leaves and twigs.

With their immensely long legs, grown-up giraffes can run for great distances without getting tired. They sway their necks from side to side as they run and have a top speed of about 47 kph. Their only enemies are lions who kill the old and sick ones for food.

A giraffe has a very awkward time getting his head down to drink. He has to spread his front legs apart, like this, and lower his neck between them. His front legs are longer than his back ones. A giraffe sucks in water and then uses his throat to squeeze it up his neck and into his stomach.

1 Baby Giraffes

A mother giraffe gives birth to her baby while she is standing up. The baby, which is born feet first, drops gently from its mother down on to the ground.

It is not often hurt by the fall and can run and walk when it is a few hours old. The baby drinks milk from teats between its mother's back legs.

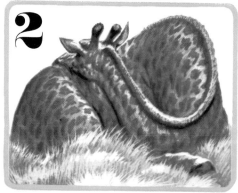

2

Big giraffes usually sleep standing up, for only a few minutes at a time. A young one may curl up on the ground to sleep, guarded by its mother.

Eyes, Ears and Noses

A giraffe has very good eyesight. His huge eyes are on the sides of his head so he can see all round him.

His hearing is very acute and he can twist his ears right round to listen to sounds from all directions.

The giraffe has special nostrils which he can close up to stop dirt and dust getting up his nose.

Fighting

These two big male giraffes are having a fight. They swing their necks together and butt each other with their heads and knobbly horns.

A giraffe's big, heavy hooves can kill a lion with a single blow.

Giraffes have two, three or four horns on top of their heads. Some have another knob which grows between their eyes.

By stretching his long neck, a big giraffe can reach leaves high up in the treetops. Acacia leaves are his favourite food. He strips them off the branches with his tongue, which is 45 cm. long, and tough hairy lips.

The Okapi

The okapi is the giraffe's only relative. Its patterned coat helps it to hide in the rain forests where it lives. Okapis were first discovered only 75 years ago.

Brown Bears

Brown Bears are found in Asia and parts of Europe. The biggest ones, Grizzlies and giant Kodiaks, live in North America.

Bears eat all kinds of food—fruit, ants, roots, honey from wild bees' nests, berries, meat and fish.

Sleeping in Winter

Most brown bears spend the cold winter months resting. They dig dens in the earth or find a quiet, warm spot, such as a cave or hollow tree to live in.

Some of the big female bears wake up in January or February to have their babies. The tiny cubs are born blind with no teeth and hardly any hair.

Playing

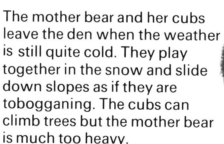

The mother bear and her cubs leave the den when the weather is still quite cold. They play together in the snow and slide down slopes as if they are tobogganing. The cubs can climb trees but the mother bear is much too heavy.

She watches them all the time to make sure that they do not get into any trouble.

1 Fishing

2

This is a giant Kodiak bear. Usually he walks about on all four legs. Sometimes, to show how big and strong he is, he stands up on his back legs, like this.

This mother bear is teaching her cubs how to catch a fish to eat. They are standing very quietly in the shallow water waiting for one to swim by.

When she sees a fish, the bear quickly grabs it in her huge paw and puts it into her mouth. Sometimes she will flip a fish out on to the bank.

8

Polar Bears

Polar Bears live on the cold icy shores of the Arctic ocean. In winter they live where the pack-ice meets the sea.

They are one of the biggest and strongest animals in the world. Standing on its back legs, a polar bear is taller than most elephants.

The females dig dens in the snow to have their babies in. The cubs stay with their mother for about ten months.

A polar bear feeds mainly on meat. It catches a seal by creeping over the ice and pouncing on it while it is asleep. Sometimes it waits for one to swim up for air where the ice is broken. As soon as the seal's head pops up out of the water, the bear reaches down and bites it with his huge teeth. He then hauls it out of the water on to the ice to eat it.

Keeping Warm

A polar bear has a thick, shaggy coat and a layer of fat under his skin to keep him warm. Hairs on the bottom of his feet stop him sliding about on the ice.

In the Water

Baby polar bears do not seem to like the cold water at first. By the time they are six months old, they are expert swimmers and follow their mother about in the water.

Sometimes they rest their heads on her back if they are very tired. When swimming, polar bears use their front legs to paddle with and they steer with their back legs.

Other Bears

This is a spectacled bear. He has this name because of the white fur around his eyes. It makes him look as if he is wearing glasses. He lives in South America.

The sun bear is the smallest kind of bear and has a very long tongue. He often tears open trees with his claws to lick the honey out of the wild bees' nests.

Sloth bears will sleep almost anywhere and they snore loudly. Baby ones ride around on their mother's back, clinging to her shaggy fur with their long claws.

Tigers

Tigers are found in many countries in Asia. Some live in steamy jungles and swamps. Others live in cold mountain country.

Like most big cats, they spend the day resting and sleeping. At night they hunt for food.

A grown-up male tiger is the biggest cat in the world. The female, who is called a tigress, is smaller and lighter than the male.

A tiger's striped coat is a good camouflage. It makes it very difficult to see in long grass, shady places and in moonlight when it is hunting.

Tiger cubs are born in a den. They are quite helpless until they are about two months old. Until then, they are looked after and fed by their mother.

Growing Up

A tigress usually has three or four babies at the same time. At first they drink her milk to make them strong. The father tiger does not help look after the cubs. He leaves the tigress to teach them all the things they need to know. The cubs fight and play with each other and their mother.

They practise how to stalk and pounce. Soon they must kill for themselves. By the time they are two years old they will be expert hunters.

1 Tiger Talk

2

Tigers talk to each other by roaring. A male roars to tell other tigers to keep away. A tigress roars to call to her cubs or to attract a male.

A big male tiger lives by himself on a special, large piece of land known as his territory. He marks it by spraying urine over the trees and bushes.

He also leaves droppings and scrapes grooves in the ground. This lets other tigers know that the land belongs to him and warns them to keep away.

he cubs hide in caves or thick scrub and grass while their mother goes off hunting for food. When she has killed an animal, she brings back the meat.

When the cubs are about three months old, the mother leads them to the meat. She makes a den nearby so that they can eat when they are hungry.

After they have eaten as much as they can, the cubs rest in the den. When the mother kills more food, she leads them to it and makes another den for them.

Keeping Cool

Tigers hate being too hot and often sit in shallow water to cool down. They are good swimmers and sometimes catch fish and turtles to eat.

Keeping Warm

In very cold places, tigers grow thick, shaggy coats to keep themselves warm. They are usually bigger than the jungle tigers.

Their coats are paler with fewer stripes than other tigers. A grown-up male, like this one, has a ruff of long hair round his face.

3

If he is very angry, a tiger wrinkles up his nose, snarls and twists his ears round to show two white spots. This is a warning to keep away from him.

4

A tiger flicks his tail from side to side when he is stalking an animal. He lashes it about as he charges and pounces. It shows that he is very excited.

The tiger swallows his food in big chunks without bothering to chew it properly. Sometimes he eats so much, he does not have to feed again for several days.

Rhinos

Two kinds of rhino live in Africa—black rhinos and the bigger white rhinos. Both are really a greyish-brown colour, but the black ones are slightly darker.

They look alike, with thick leathery skin and two big curved horns growing just behind their noses. Their mouths and heads are a different shape.

Rhinos usually live near to water. They move about and feed during the night when it is cool. They sleep either standing up or lying down during the day.

Feeding Together

A Black Rhino's Mouth

Black rhinos have rubbery, pointed lips for plucking leaves off bushes.

A White Rhino's Mouth

White rhinos have wide, flat mouths made specially for grazing off the ground.

Black and white rhinos sometimes feed together in the same place. They never fight over food because they like different things to eat.

The black rhino eats the leaves, twigs and shoots of small bushes. The white one eats only grass. His neck is longer because he has to bend down to get his food.

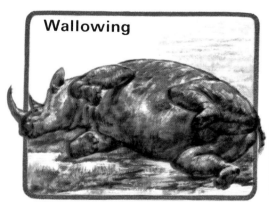

Wallowing

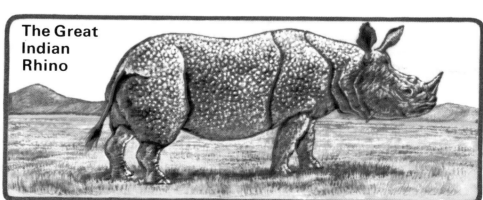

The Great Indian Rhino

This rhino is having a mud bath. Every day rhinos wallow in muddy pools to keep cool and get rid of insects. Sometimes they roll over on their backs, like this.

This kind of rhino lives in India, sleeping and feeding in tall elephant grass or swampy jungles. His thick, bumpy skin is folded in places and makes him

look as if he is wearing a suit of armour. Unlike African rhinos, he only has one horn. Indian rhinos fight only with their teeth and do not use their horns.

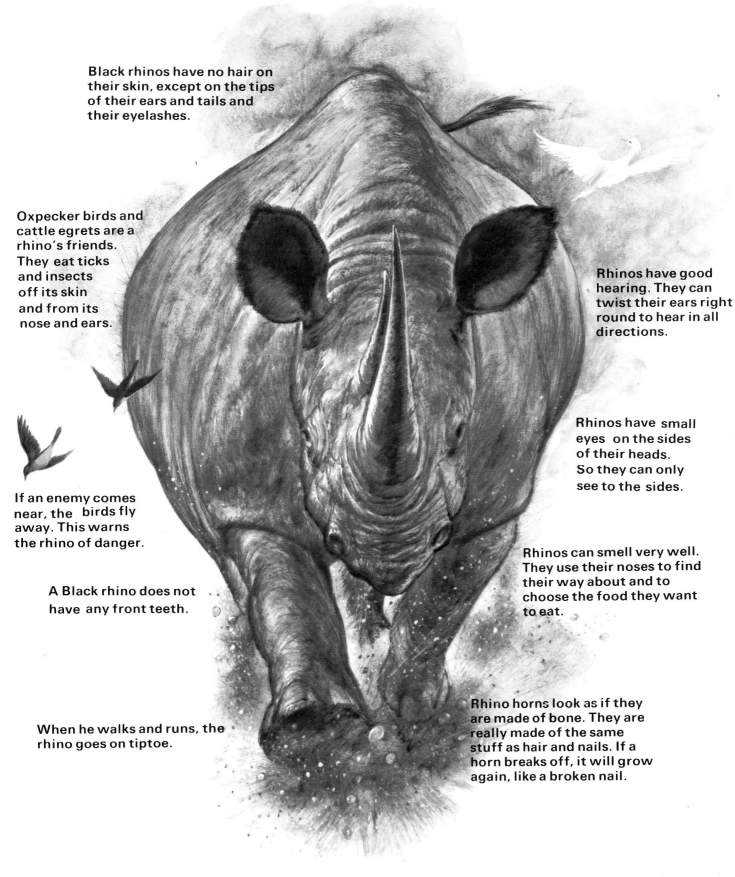

Black rhinos have no hair on their skin, except on the tips of their ears and tails and their eyelashes.

Oxpecker birds and cattle egrets are a rhino's friends. They eat ticks and insects off its skin and from its nose and ears.

Rhinos have good hearing. They can twist their ears right round to hear in all directions.

If an enemy comes near, the birds fly away. This warns the rhino of danger.

Rhinos have small eyes on the sides of their heads. So they can only see to the sides.

A Black rhino does not have any front teeth.

Rhinos can smell very well. They use their noses to find their way about and to choose the food they want to eat.

Rhino horns look as if they are made of bone. They are really made of the same stuff as hair and nails. If a horn breaks off, it will grow again, like a broken nail.

When he walks and runs, the rhino goes on tiptoe.

Most black rhinos seem to have bad tempers. They charge when they are frightened or become suspicious. This is probably because they cannot see very well ahead of them.

They grunt and squeal when they are excited. This black rhino is charging an enemy. He uses his ears and nose to hear and smell where the danger is and they help him to go the right way.

Rhinos can gallop round corners and change direction very quickly, although they are so heavy and bulky. They can run very fast—sometimes at 45 kph. over a short distance.

Sloths, Anteaters and Armadillos

These strange animals live in South America. They all use their strong, curved claws to defend themselves against their enemies.

A sloth also uses his claws to hang from the branches of trees. He reaches out with long arms to collect the food he wants to eat.

Anteaters and armadillos feed on ants and termites. Sometimes an armadillo catches snakes, worms and spiders to eat. Sloths prefer fruit and leaves.

Sloths

Sloths are the slowest furry animals in the world. They spend their lives moving lazily along the branches of trees or just hanging upside-down asleep.

They never clean themselves or move unless they have to and they even sneeze slowly. Sloths eat, sleep and have babies while they are upside-down.

As soon as the baby is born, it grips tightly to its mother's fur with its tiny claws. The mother sloth carries her baby about on her chest, like this.

Sloths cannot stand up on their arms and legs. It is very difficult for them to move on the ground at all. Out of a tree a sloth is completely helpless.

This one is trying to crawl to the nearest tree. It might take him hours to reach it. He drags himself along on his stomach, using his long, front claws.

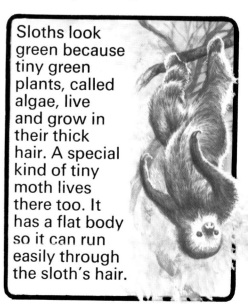

Sloths look green because tiny green plants, called algae, live and grow in their thick hair. A special kind of tiny moth lives there too. It has a flat body so it can run easily through the sloth's hair.

Anteaters

The Giant Anteater

Giant anteaters always seem to have their long snouts close to the ground, sniffing for food. They have to walk on their knuckles, like this, to protect their long, sharp claws.

This baby anteater will ride about on its mother's back until it is about a year old. When she is ready to have another baby, it will go off and live by itself.

A giant anteater usually takes off at a slow, clumsy gallop when it sees an enemy. If it is forced to fight, it rears up on its back legs and lashes out with its claws.

Tamanduas

A tamandua is a small anteater that spends most of its life in trees. Like other anteaters, its favourite foods are ants, termites and squashy grubs.

Tamanduas tear open anthills and termite mounds with their sharp, front claws. Then they poke their snouts into the holes to catch the insects.

This tamandua has collected lots of ants on his long, sticky tongue. He shoots it in and out of the ants' nests to catch them and put them into his mouth.

Armadillos

1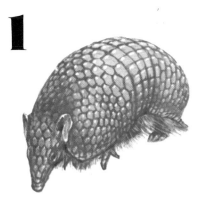

2

Armadillos are covered with lots of bony plates, which protect them like armour. This giant one is digging a burrow with its claws.

The small, three-banded armadillo walks about on the tips of its strong, front claws. It has a very good way of protecting itself.

If it is frightened, it rolls itself up into a tight ball, about the size of a melon. Only its enemy, a jaguar, is strong enough to rip the ball apart.

Elephants

Elephants are the biggest land animals. There are two kinds, the African elephant and the Indian one. These two pages are all about African elephants.

If an elephant gets too hot, it flaps its huge ears backwards and forwards to cool itself down.

Elephants have very strong teeth to chew branches and roots of trees. They grow six sets of teeth in a lifetime. New teeth grow as the old ones are worn down.

Elephants live in small family groups called clans. In each clan there are a few grown-up female elephants, their babies and teenage children, and other young elephants.

The oldest and biggest female is the leader of the clan. Big bull elephants live by themselves or in their own groups. They join the females at mating time.

A mother leaves the clan to have her baby. One or two elephants may go with her. After the baby is born, she helps it to stand by lifting it up with her feet and trunk

Mud Baths

Every day elephants roll about in the mud, like this, to get rid of insects and to keep their skin in good condition.

After a mud bath, elephants suck dust and sand up their trunks and then blow it out to stick it to their muddy bodies.

Then they rub themselves against a termite hill or a big tree. This squashes any insects which are left on their skin.

16

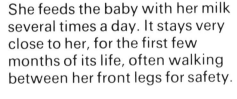

She feeds the baby with her milk several times a day. It stays very close to her, for the first few months of its life, often walking between her front legs for safety.

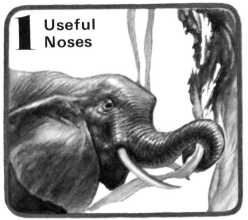

1 Useful Noses

An elephant's trunk is a very useful thing. He uses it to pick berries, gather tufts of grass, tear down leaves and branches and strip bark off trees.

2

He also uses his trunk for drinking. He sucks up water through the two long nostrils and squirts it into his mouth. A trunk holds about 2 litres.

3

This elephant is using his trunk as a snorkel so he can breathe under the water. He also smells, feels and breathes with it when he is out of the water.

4

Elephants lift heavy things and push big trees over with their trunks. They scoop out holes, dig for water and even rub their eyes with their long noses.

Fighting

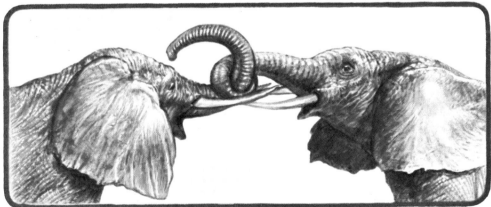

Bull elephants often fight each other at mating time. They use their trunks and tusks as weapons, to hit and jab each other. Tusks are really very long teeth.

The fights do not last very long. The elephants stop as soon as one proves he will win. He then goes off to mate with a female elephant, called a cow.

Indian Elephants

Indian elephants are not as big as African ones. They have smaller ears and tusks and only one lip on the end of their trunks. African elephants have two.

17

Beavers

1 Baby Beavers

Inside the lodge, the mother beaver lies on a soft bed of bark and twigs to have her babies. The tiny kits are covered with soft brown fur.

2

Kits can walk at birth but they have to practice a lot before they become expert swimmers. This mother beaver is holding a kit's tail to steer it in the right direction.

3

When a baby beaver is very tired, its mother may help it back to the lodge. She carries it in her arms, like this, or picks it up by the scruff of its neck with her mouth.

Beavers are excellent builders. They make their houses, called beaver lodges, on the edges of lakes and rivers.
Like rats, mice, rabbits and squirrels, beavers are rodents. All rodents have two big, sharp front teeth to gnaw with.

Mother and father beavers stay together all their lives. They have three or four babies, which are called kits, every year.
A young beaver lives with its parents until it is about two years old. Then it goes off alone to start a family and build a lodge of its own.

Beavers eat the bark, twigs, branches and leaves of trees. They like aspen, birch and willow trees the best.

Beavers bite down trees with their sharp teeth to get food and to make their lodges. They sit on their broad, flat tails to gnaw at a tree trunk.

A beaver's teeth grow all the time as they get worn down by gnawing. If they grew too long, they might prop open its mouth.

These two beavers are grooming each other with their teeth and claws. They have a special split claw on their back feet for combing through fur.

All summer, the beavers collect food and put it in the foodstore for the cold winter months.

Beavers are very good swimmers. They paddle with their webbed back feet and use their flat tails as rudders to steer.

Grooming

A beaver has oil glands at the base of its tail. It grooms itself to spread oil over its coat to make itself waterproof. At first, baby beavers get very wet whenever they swim. Their mother teaches them how to oil their coats. This beaver knows just what to do.

1 First it cleans its nose with its front paws.

2 Then it scratches its head, chest, arms and stomach.

3 It leaves the cleaning of its legs and back until last.

Beavers put their food into their mouths with their front paws.

Beavers are always scurrying about finding sticks and twigs to repair their lodges.

This beaver is slapping its tail on the water to warn the others of danger. It makes a very loud noise.

The beavers chop the tree into pieces and drag or roll them, one by one, to the place where they are building the lodge.

Big beavers bunch lots of twigs together and bite off the leaves. Baby beavers eat one twig at a time.

A Beaver Lodge

The lodge is made of sticks and twigs, packed together with mud and stones.

Before they make their lodges, beavers build a dam of sticks to make the water deeper.

The beaver family live in one big room above the water. A hole in the roof lets air in and out of the lodge.

All the entrances are under the water to stop other animals getting into the lodge. The beavers store their food close to one of the entrances.

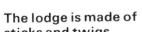

Lions

The lion is called the king of beasts because he is so fierce and powerful.

Lions are the only wild cats that live together in family groups. A family of lions is called a pride.

In each pride there are two or three grown-up lions, five or six grown-up lionesses and lots of cubs. There may also be several young lions and some lionesses.

Family Life

Cubs chase about and spring on each other's tails. They learn to do things, like stalking and pouncing, which will be useful when they have to look after themselves and catch their food.

They play with their mother and nuzzle her face. This keeps her friendly and stops her from getting cross and hurting them. Their father does not play with them very much.

1 The Head of the Family

Grown-up lions have big, shaggy manes round their heads and necks. This one is roaring to warn all the other lions to keep away from his pride.

2

If another lion comes too close, then they will fight. The fight goes on until one of them is hurt and runs away. Sometimes two or three younger lions will attack an older lion all together.

1 The Kill

The lionesses do most of the hunting. Sometimes they hunt alone but usually two or three hunt together. Zebras and gnus are their favourite food.

2

First they stalk an animal, keeping well hidden. Then they rush out and spring on it. A lioness can make a spring of over 10 metres through the air.

3

She sinks her fangs into the animal's throat to kill it. Sometimes she will drag the body to a sheltered place where the pride can feed on the meat.

20

The cubs are much more lively than the big lions. They play and explore even when it is very hot. Their mother leaves them hidden in the bushes and long grass while she goes off to hunt. Their spotted coats make them very difficult for an enemy to see.

The cubs start eating meat before they are three months old. After a year, they are able to hunt and kill for themselves.

4 The big lions usually eat first while the rest of the family watches. If the animal is only small and they are very hungry the big lions may eat it all.

5 But if the kill is big, there will be enough for the whole pride. The lionesses and cubs wait until the lions have had enough before they start to eat.

6 As soon as the whole pride has left the kill, hyenas, jackals and vultures come to finish it off. They pick every single scrap of meat off the bones.

Zebras

Zebras live in small family herds which are usually led by one big, strong male. He is called a stallion. Female zebras are called mares and baby ones, foals.

They are fat and healthy because they normally have enough to eat. They like the coarse, stringy grass that other animals will not touch. Herds of zebra are often seen grazing peacefully with giraffes, wildebeests and ostriches.

There are usually five or six mares and their foals in each family group. The stallion protects them and keeps all the other stallions away.

If he is alarmed, he gives a loud bark to warn his herd of danger and they gallop off. He will even fight young lions if they attack the group.

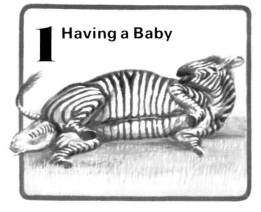

1 Having a Baby

The mother zebra lies down in a quiet spot to have her baby. It is born inside a big bag full of water, called the birth sac. The foal's head comes out first.

2

The baby struggles out of the birth sac as soon as it is born. Its mother, who is very tired now, lifts up her head and licks it dry.

3

At first it is very wobbly on its legs and it falls over a lot. But when it is about 15 minutes old, the foal is steady enough to walk with its mother to join the herd.

Zebras like to stay close to each other in small groups. They often rest, standing in pairs like this, during the hottest part of the day.

They groom each other to get rid of ticks and other itchy insects. The zebras use their teeth to bite the insects off one another's skin.

Grown-up male zebras fight a lot, especially during the mating season. They gallop round and round, kicking and biting each other's legs and necks.

Bush-babies

Bush-babies are small furry animals with long back legs and huge eyes. They move very fast among the trees and can jump over 4 metres from branch to branch. Small kinds of bush-babies hop along the ground like kangaroos, using their tails to balance.

They are called bush-babies because the noise they make sounds just like a human baby crying. They are also known as galagos.

All bush-babies are nocturnal. This means that they rest in the daytime and feed at night. Their enormous eyes help them to see in the dim light.

At dawn, bush-babies chatter together before they go to sleep. At night, they search for food. They catch insects with their hands and collect fruit and birds' eggs to eat.

This mother bush-baby hides her baby in the trees when she goes off to feed. The baby can already cling to branches with its long fingers and toes.

Other Night Animals

Lorises move about very slowly and never jump. They sleep with their heads tucked between all four feet. This baby slender loris is following its mother.

The aye-aye is a very rare animal, about the size of a cat. It has a special thin middle finger on each hand. It pokes this finger into holes to catch insects.

The tiny tarsier can swivel its head right round, like this, to watch out for danger. It uses its tail as a brake when it makes huge leaps from tree to tree.

Red Foxes

Red foxes live mainly in woods and bushy country. But some have learned to find food in towns, eating rats, mice and the scraps thrown into dustbins.

During the winter, red foxes have long, thick fur to keep them warm. They look much thinner in the summer when they lose their winter coats. Their big, bushy tails are called brushes and usually have white or black tips.

1 Growing Up

Red foxes live in dens, called earths. These may be under fallen trees, in hedges or on hillsides. They are often old warrens and burrows which were dug out by rabbits or badgers.

Female red foxes are called vixens. They have their babies in the earths during the spring. Usually four or five tiny cubs, covered with dark brown fluffy fur, are born.

When the cubs are about two weeks old, their eyes open and they begin to explore. They sniff and scratch at everything and tumble about the den.

After about six weeks, the cubs lose their baby fur and start to look more like their parents. Now they are more daring and go outside the earth to play.

They stalk and pounce on each other and on sticks and stones. When they are about six months old, they will be big enough to catch food for themselves.

Poaching

Farmers do not like foxes much because the foxes sometimes eat their turkeys and chickens. This fox has found a wild duck's nest and is eating the eggs.

1 Hunting

Red foxes eat rats, mice, rabbits, frogs and insects. While the vixen looks after the cubs, the father fox, called a dog fox, goes off to hunt for food.

2

He is a very silent hunter. When he sees something to catch he keeps absolutely still. Then he pounces on it. This fox is taking a mouse back to his family.

Giant Pandas

Giant pandas live in China, high up on the mountain plateaux in the dense bamboo forests. It is very cold there but the panda's thick, rough hair helps to keep it warm.

A baby panda, like the one in the picture on the right, cannot move around on his own. He will start to crawl when he is about three months old. His mother takes great care of him. She makes sure he is always clean and has enough to eat.

Big pandas are very good at climbing. They will scramble up the nearest tree to get away from their enemies—leopards and wolves. Sometimes they sleep up trees, comfortably wedged between the branches.

Most pandas spend the whole day eating. Their favourite food is bamboo but they also like to eat other things, such as bamboo rats, small birds, snakes, flowers and fish. This one is feasting on a tasty bamboo shoot.

Wildebeests

Wildebeests are very strange looking antelopes with hairy faces, and beards which grow under their chins. They have long legs and run very fast. They are also called gnus.

There are more wildebeests living on the grassy African plains than any other kind of animal. But a lot of them are killed by hungry lions, hyenas and other meat-eating animals. Many die of a disease called rinderpest.

Little insects called bot-flies often lay their eggs in a gnu's nose. Usually he manages to sneeze the eggs out. But sometimes they hatch into flies inside his nose.

The flies bore their way into the gnu's brain and make him lose his balance. He turns round and round until he is so dizzy and exhausted that he falls over and dies. This is called 'turning disease'.

Hyenas lurk close to the gnus with turning disease. They wait for a gnu to fall over and then they kill and eat him.

If a wildebeest is upset or frightened he behaves in a very curious way. He prances about, paws the ground, thrashes his long tail about and pokes his horns into the earth.

Some wildebeests drown when they have to swim across deep, wide rivers on the way to their new feeding places.

During their march across the plains, gnus often walk in single file. They make deep tracks in the dry soil and kick up huge clouds of dust as they go.

Wildebeests do not seem to be very clever animals. They sometimes seem to forget where they are going. If one wildebeest starts walking in the wrong direction, others will follow him.

Often two big bull gnus fight over females they both want for their harem. They drop down on their knees, like this, and jab each other with their sharp horns.

Each grown-up male, or bull gnu, chooses the females he wants as mates. They are called his harem. He gallops round them, keeping them in a group away from other bulls.

Thousands of gnus wander across the Serengeti plains in East Africa. During the rainy season they live in scattered herds and grow fat from feeding on the lush grass. When the rains end, the grass quickly dries up and goes brown. Then the gnus have to move to new grazing places where there is plenty of water for them to drink and fresh grass. They gather together and move, like a huge army, across the plains. Year after year, they follow the same trails. This mass movement is called migration. When the rainy season begins again, the gnus go back to their old feeding places. The females then have their babies.

27

Cape Hunting Dogs

Cape hunting dogs are very fierce and savage. They live together on the open plains of Africa in groups of up to 20 animals, called packs.

The dogs wander from place to place hunting for food. They will stay in one spot if there are plenty of animals, such as zebras or gnus to kill.

No two dogs have exactly the same markings on their coats. Only their tails are the same— with white tufts of hair on the ends.

1 The Kill

In the early morning or at dusk, most of the pack go off to hunt for food. A few stay behind to look after the young puppies.

The dogs walk silently towards a herd of animals and then start to chase it. The herd rushes off when it sees the dogs coming.

Soon one animal, usually ill or weak, is separated from the herd. The dogs chase it until it is too tired to run any more.

2

The animal has a horrible death as it is eaten alive by the savage dogs. Some of them attack its face. Others bite and snap chunks of meat from its rump and legs.

The dogs eat quickly before any hyenas and jackals come to steal their food. They hunt every day, often killing far more animals then they can eat.

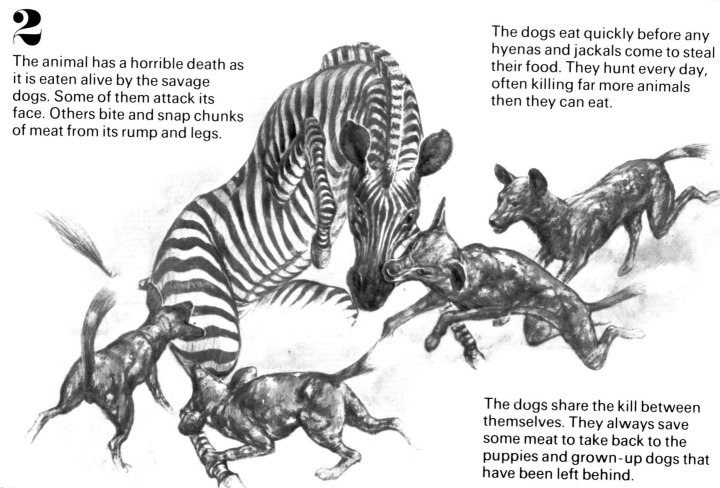

The dogs share the kill between themselves. They always save some meat to take back to the puppies and grown-up dogs that have been left behind.

1 Growing Up

Baby hunting dogs are born in burrows which have been left empty by other animals. The mother dog, known as a bitch, may have as many as twelve pups at the same time.

2

The puppies start eating meat when they are two weeks old. Their mother sicks up food she has swallowed to feed them. They squeak, wag their tails and nuzzle her mouth to beg for more.

3

When the pack moves to a new hunting ground, the puppies go too. The big dogs pick them up gently by the scruffs of their necks to carry them there. The herds move on when the dogs come.

Other Wild Dogs

Wolves also live and hunt in packs. A wolf pack is a family, with father as the leader, mother and, probably, the cubs from the last litter.

These two big male wolves are fighting to see which is the next leader after father. The loser has rolled over on his back to show he is beaten.

Coyotes usually live and hunt alone. In the evenings, they often meet on the prairies and howl together in chorus. From a distance, it sounds just as if they are singing together.

Dingoes are dogs which live in Australia. They were once tame dogs which escaped and bred in the wild. Sometimes they kill kangaroos and wallabies.

Hyenas and jackals hunt and kill when it gets dark. They do not like each other much. When they meet they often fight over bones and scraps of food.

During the day, jackals lurk in the shadows waiting to steal food. They are scavengers. A scavenger clears up the left-overs of another animal's kill.

Camels

There are two kinds of camels. One kind has two humps and is called the Bactrian camel. It lives in the Gobi desert in Asia. The other, the Arabian camel, which is called a dromedary, has one hump.

Camels eat all sorts of desert grasses and salty plants. If they get very hungry they will also eat meat, bones and skin. There are very few wild camels left in the world now. Most of them are tame and are used to carry heavy loads.

Floppy Humps

When a camel has not had enough to eat, his humps shrink and flop over to one side, like this.

When camels are well-fed, their humps are plump and solid like these ones.

Camels store fat in their humps. It gives them lots of energy. Their humps also help to protect them from the heat of the sun.

Camels never clean themselves and are always very smelly. They are sick at you if you annoy them.

Camels can close up their nostrils to stop sand and dust getting up their noses.

A camel has a big split in the middle of its upper lip. There is a groove from each nostril to the split, so that any dribble from its nose goes straight into its mouth and is not wasted.

A camel has hard leathery pads of skin on its front and back legs to rest on when it kneels down.

Soft fleshy pads on the bottom of its feet stop the camel from sinking into the soft sand dunes.

The two toes on each foot have big hard nails and are joined together by a tough bit of skin.

Camels are very well suited to desert life. They are able to live in hot, dry places because they can go without a drink of water for many days.

This picture of a Bactrian camel shows you some of the special parts of its body that help it to stay alive in the hot and cold deserts and on mountains.

Winters in the Gobi desert are very cold. To keep themselves warm, Bactrian camels grow thick woolly coats. In the summer this hair falls out.

Dromedaries

Arabian camels often make long journeys across the desert carrying heavy loads. Sometimes they have little to eat and drink for days.

Although a camel does not sweat very much, it loses some water through its breath and urine. At the end of a long journey it is often thin and weak.

These camels have come to a water-hole in the desert and are very thirsty. They may drink as much as 20 big buckets of water at a time.

Camels' Relatives

Vicuna

Guanaco

Alpaca

Llama

These animals are all relatives of the camel but none of them has a hump or lives in the desert. Vicunas and guanacos live in the wild in small herds.

They eat the green grass high up on the Andes mountains. Alpacas are tame and covered in valuable wool which sometimes grows all down their legs.

The wool is used to make very expensive cloth. Llamas are tame and have been trained to carry heavy loads. They are also kept for their milk and wool.

Kangaroos

Red kangaroos are one of the biggest and best-known kinds of kangaroo. They live on the inland plains over most of Australia. The herds are called mobs. The head of the mob is known as the old man.

Grown-up males are about 1.5 metres tall and usually a reddish-brown colour. Females are smaller with blue-grey coats. They have pouches low down on their stomachs for their babies.

How a Baby Kangaroo is Born

Just before the baby is born, the mother licks the inside of her pouch to clean it. She also licks the fur on her stomach. Then she sits like this to give birth.

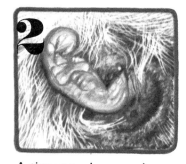

A tiny newborn red kangaroo is about the size of a man's thumb nail. It is completely blind, has no hair and does not look like a kangaroo at all.

It grips its mother's hair with the claws on its front feet and crawls up her stomach and into her pouch. This only takes the baby about three minutes.

The baby stays in the pouch and sucks milk from the teats until it is fully formed. After about seven months, it is big enough to jump about and feed on its own.

32

Young kangaroos are called joeys. A joey goes on drinking his mother's milk for six months after leaving her pouch. This one has popped his head in to have a drink.

Until he gets too big, the joey often goes back to the pouch whenever he is tired or frightened. He jumps in head first and turns a complete somersault. Only his head and legs stick out.

A big kangaroo can make a jump of 3 metres in the air and 9 metres along. He springs off his strong back legs. His tail helps him to balance. The faster he goes, the further he jumps.

When male kangaroos fight, they rear up on their tails, and hold on to each other with their front feet. They give powerful kicks with their back feet. Their sharp claws can make very deep wounds.

Kangaroos spend most of the day sunbathing. When it gets cooler in the evening, they start to look for food and water. Red kangaroos can go without water for several days.

Other Animals with Pouches

Female koalas have upside-down pouches which open between their back legs. The babies crawl into them after they are born. Koalas live in eucalyptus trees and feed on the leaves and bark.

Animals that have pouches to carry their babies in are called marsupials. Only the females have them. This baby long-nosed bandicoot is trying to get into his mother's upside-down pouch.

Baby Virginian opossums ride about on their mother's backs after leaving the pouches. Sometimes, when opossums are frightened or hurt, they pretend to be dead so that their enemies leave them alone.

Bats

Bats are the only furry animals that can fly. There are about 1000 different kinds living all over the world. During the day, they rest in dark caves, hollow trees and empty buildings or hang from the branches of trees.

As they rest, bats clean themselves with their toes and tongues. At night, they fly about looking for food. Grown-up female bats usually have one baby every year. The baby clings to its mother with its teeth.

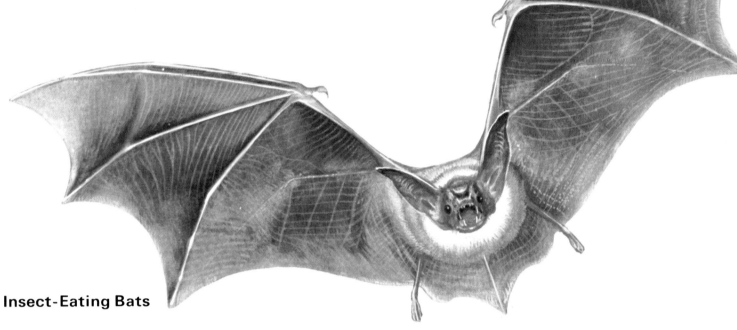

Insect-Eating Bats

A bat's wings are made of very thin, stretchy skin which grows between its long, bony fingers and its legs and tail. The back feet, with their sharp, curved claws, are free for grasping things.

This brown bat likes eating insects. It catches them while it flies about. Insect-eating bats have sharp teeth to scrunch up their food.

After a meal of many insects, the bat finds somewhere to rest. It hangs by its toes and folds up its wings. When it gets hungry again at dusk it goes off to hunt for more insects.

Catching Insects

Winter Sleep

Bats make high-pitched squeaks to catch flying insects and to find their way in the dark. The echoes of their squeaks tell them exactly where things are (a).

The bat catches the insect with its wings (b). It then pokes its head down to get the insect into its mouth. If it is a large insect, the bat will land to eat it.

Some bats sleep throughout the cold winter months. They hang upside-down, like this, and fold their wings round their bodies. This bat is covered with dew.

34

Fish-Eating Bats

At dusk, the fish-eating bat comes out of his hiding place to look for food. He flies very slowly above the water, swooping down to catch tiny fish with his sharp, hooked claws. As soon as the bat catches a fish, he lifts it out of the water and puts it into his mouth.

Vampire Bats

A vampire bat feeds only on fresh blood. He usually attacks an animal while it is asleep. The bat bites open the skin and laps up the blood with his long tongue. It is so quiet that the animal does not even wake up. Sometimes, vampire bats drink so much blood they cannot fly for several hours.

Flower-Feeding Bats

Flower-feeding bats are usually small with pointed heads and very long tongues. This one is poking its tongue down a flower to find something to eat. It hovers beside the flower. The pollen and nectar in flowers are the bat's favourite foods. They stick to the tiny hairs on the top of its tongue as it feeds.

Fruit-Eating Bats

These big bats are also called flying foxes because they have such fox-like faces. They eat ripe fruit, like bananas, wild figs, paw-paws and pineapples. Fruit bats often squabble and fight each other. They lash out with their claws and snap with their teeth. They fly out to eat at dusk and spend several hours feeding and resting on the fruit trees.

Leopards

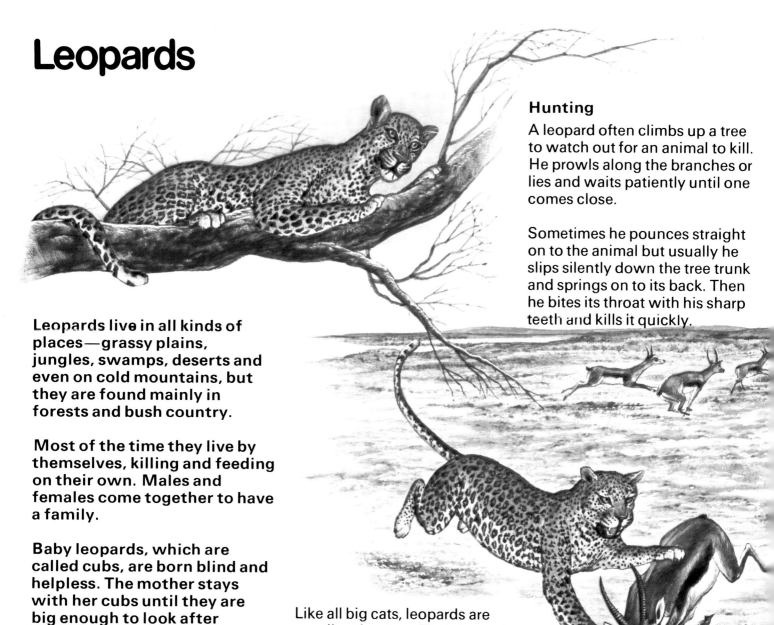

Hunting

A leopard often climbs up a tree to watch out for an animal to kill. He prowls along the branches or lies and waits patiently until one comes close.

Sometimes he pounces straight on to the animal but usually he slips silently down the tree trunk and springs on to its back. Then he bites its throat with his sharp teeth and kills it quickly.

Leopards live in all kinds of places—grassy plains, jungles, swamps, deserts and even on cold mountains, but they are found mainly in forests and bush country.

Most of the time they live by themselves, killing and feeding on their own. Males and females come together to have a family.

Baby leopards, which are called cubs, are born blind and helpless. The mother stays with her cubs until they are big enough to look after themselves and catch and kill their own food.

Like all big cats, leopards are excellent hunters. Their favourite kinds of food are small antelopes, wild pigs, baboons and porcupines.

Before the Kill

Leopards need to keep their claws sharp for climbing trees and killing animals.

This one has found a very good scratching post. It is sharpening its claws on the bark of a tree before it goes hunting for food.

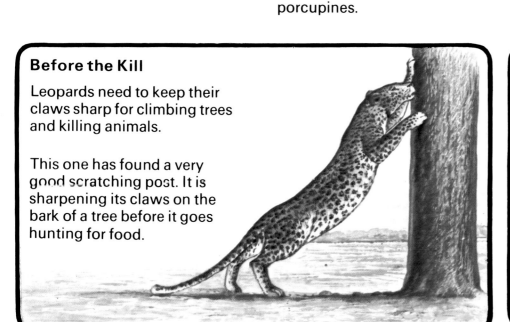

After the Meal

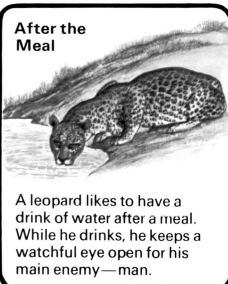

A leopard likes to have a drink of water after a meal. While he drinks, he keeps a watchful eye open for his main enemy—man.

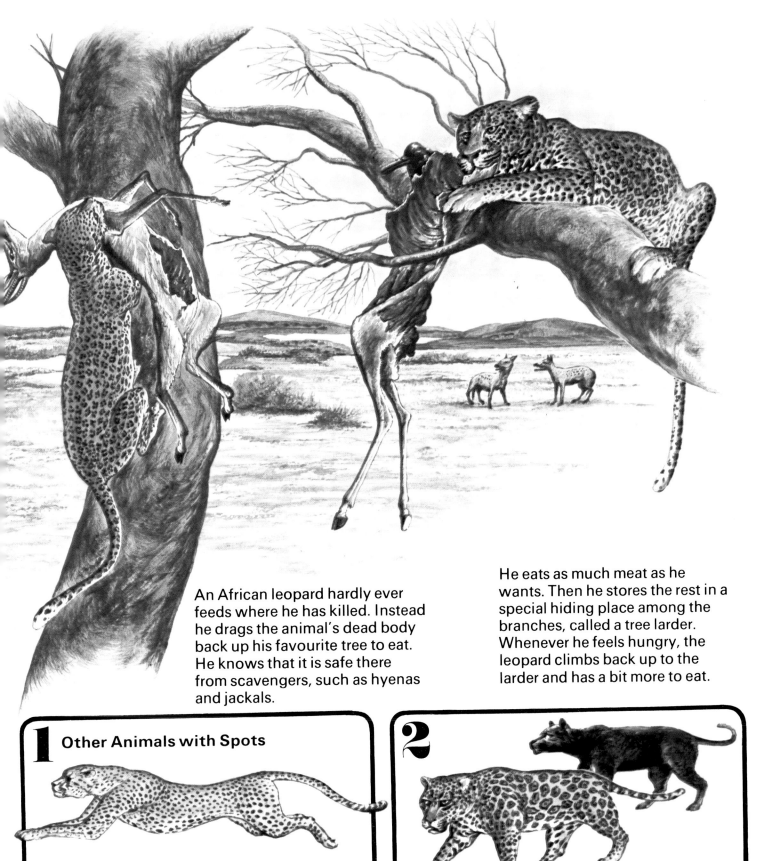

An African leopard hardly ever feeds where he has killed. Instead he drags the animal's dead body back up his favourite tree to eat. He knows that it is safe there from scavengers, such as hyenas and jackals.

He eats as much meat as he wants. Then he stores the rest in a special hiding place among the branches, called a tree larder. Whenever he feels hungry, the leopard climbs back up to the larder and has a bit more to eat.

1 Other Animals with Spots

2

Cheetahs are the fastest animals in the world and can run at over 110 kph. They are smaller and thinner than leopards and have longer legs. Unlike most big cats, they stalk and sprint after their prey to catch it.

Jaguars are stronger and fatter than leopards and their spots are a different shape. Indian leopards are called panthers. Sometimes they look completely black but really they have very dark spots all over their coats.

Red Deer

Red deer spend most of the day resting quietly in the shade. In the evening, they move to their favourite feeding places to eat leaves and grass.

Deer eat lots of food very quickly without bothering to chew it properly. While they are resting they bring the food back up into their mouths and chew it over and over again. This is called chewing the cud.

Grown-up male red deer are called stags and the females are known as hinds. Only the stags have big, bony antlers on their heads. Young red deer are called calves.

The deer's summer coats are sleek and red. In the winter they grow much thicker and turn a pale greyish-brown colour. Most red deer have a white patch under their tails. Other deer follow this when one scents danger and dashes away.

A Baby Red Deer

This baby deer is only a few hours old but he can already stand up and walk a little. Until he grows a bit older and stronger, he will rest, hidden in the grass and ferns.

The spots on his furry coat make him very difficult for an enemy to see. His mother feeds him several times a day on her milk. Soon she will take him to join the other hinds and their calves in the herd.

1 How Antlers Grow

A year-old male deer is called a knobber because he has two hairy knobs on the front of his head. His antlers will start to grow from these knobs when he is about two years old.

2

Every spring the antlers fall off. When they grow again in the summer, they are a bit bigger than the last ones. At first, they are covered with soft skin and hair, called velvet.

3

In the autumn, the velvet peels off, leaving a hard, bony part. Sometimes a stag rubs the velvet off against a tree. Fully-grown antlers, like these ones, have six or more spikes.

1 The Mating Season

The mating season, called the rut, begins in the autumn. Each stag rounds up the hinds he wants as his wives. He bellows to tell other stags to keep away.

2

The rut is a very tiring time for the stag. He is always rushing about trying to keep all his hinds close together in a group. They are called his harem.

He mates with each of them so that they will have babies in the early summer. Hardly any time is left for him to eat so he gets very thin and worn out.

3

During the rut, which lasts for about six weeks, a stag fights any other stag which comes near his harem of hinds.

The two stags lock their antlers together and try to push each other backwards. When one wins, he chases the other away.

After the rut is over, the stag is very tired and is hoarse through bellowing. Now it is time to leave his harem and join other stags.

Other Deer

The Moose

A moose is the biggest kind of deer and has huge antlers. In summer, it often wades into water to eat water plants, tearing them with rubbery lips.

The Chinese Water Deer

This tiny deer is very shy and hides in long grass and reeds. Instead of antlers, the males have two sharp tusks which poke out below their upper lips.

The Reindeer

Reindeer live in very cold places but their thick coats keep them warm. They have big flat hooves so they can walk on snow. Both males and females have antlers.

Hippos

Hippos live in Africa and spend up to 16 hours a day lazing about in rivers and swamps. They feed all the time on waterweed.

They are the second heaviest land animals and weigh so much that they cannot jump off the ground at all.

A big male hippo, which is called a bull, weighs about as much as 60 men. Female hippos are called cows, and babies are called calves.

Hippos can float with their bodies right under the water even though they are so big. They do this to keep cool and to stop insects biting them.

They are excellent swimmers and divers and can stay under the water for up to five minutes. A big hippo can even walk along the bottom of a lake or river.

Sometimes hippos sun-bathe on river banks. But they do not stay out of the water for very long as their skins dry up quickly in the hot sun.

Birds, such as egrets and brown hamerkops, are the hippo's friends. They peck biting insects and bits of river weed off his thick skin.

1 A Hippo's Head

A hippo's ears, eyes and nose are on the top of its flat head. It can keep most of its head under the water and still hear, see and smell very well.

2

He can see specially well in dim light and can swivel his ears round to hear in all directions. When he goes under the water, he closes his nose and ears.

This hippo looks as if he is yawning. He is really showing off his big teeth as a warning to any enemy. A hippo uses his teeth as weapons to fight with.

1 Out of the Water

Hippos spend the whole night looking for food. The bulls lead the way, the cows and calves follow. A new born baby walks just in front of its mother.

As they walk, the hippos trample down wide tracks. These tracks are called hippo trails. Night after night, they walk along the same trail searching for things to eat.

2

All healthy hippos have very big appetites. They feed on grass, leaves, roots and branches. At dawn, when they are full of food, they waddle back into the water.

3

Even though they are so heavy with such stumpy legs, hippos can run quite fast for a short way. This frightened mother and baby are rushing back to the water.

1 Baby Hippos

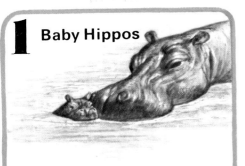

Baby hippos are born in the water. They learn to swim when they are only minutes old. Sometimes their mothers will hold their heads up out of the water.

2

Female hippos often babysit for each other. If one mother hippo wants to go off to feed or mate, she leaves her calves with another hippo.

Mud Baths

Hippos love to wallow and bask in muddy pools. They take mud baths to keep cool and to get rid of insects from their skin, just as an elephant does.

Monkeys

Monkeys usually live in family groups or big herds, called monkey troops. Most kinds spend their time feeding and sleeping in the trees.

They swing or leap from branch to branch looking for things to eat. Their favourite foods are fruit, nuts, plants and eggs.

Big, heavy monkeys like baboons prefer to live on the ground. At night they shelter near trees or rocks. They seem to be frightened of the dark.

Anubis Baboons

One strong grown-up male baboon is usually the head of the troop. All the other baboons have to obey him.

The boss baboon gets very cross if another baboon threatens him. He ruffles up his hair, bares his big teeth and barks to show he is not pleased.

Baboons mutter and grunt as they feed. They use their hands to put grass and plants into their mouths. Some baboons catch lizards, butterflies and grass-hoppers to eat.

When a baboon knows he has been defeated in a fight, he turns his rump towards the winner to show that he wants to give up.

This baby baboon is about four months old. It rides about on its mother's back like a jockey. It holds on to her fur with its fingers and toes so it does not fall off.

A baby baboon has a pink face and ears and is covered with dark fur. It stays very close to its mother, clinging to the fur on her stomach when she moves about.

These two baboons are cleaning each other. They pick and nibble bits of dirt, leaves, dry skin and salt off one another's hair and skin.

Young baboons are very playful. They chase each other about and pretend to have fights.

Baboons stay close together when they move from place to place. Some of the grown-up males walk on the outside of the troop to protect the others.

The grown-up males are very fierce and strong. They are always on the look-out for their enemies such as leopards, lions, wild dogs and hyenas.

If an enemy attacks the troop, they rush to the front to fight it off. All the other baboons quickly run away and hide among the rocks and trees.

Spider, woolly and squirrel monkeys live high up in the trees in the forests of South America.

Their long tails help the spider and woolly monkey to balance and to grip on to branches.

Spider monkeys often hang by their long, curly tails so they can reach out for fruit. Sometimes they use their tails to pick up things. They are very acrobatic and swing quickly through the branches of the trees.

Woolly monkeys can stand up on their back legs and walk along branches like tightrope walkers. They balance with their arms and tails. Usually, a woolly monkey sleeps curled up with his tail wrapped round his body.

Squirrel monkeys are very noisy and inquisitive. They chatter in the tree-tops as they leap from branch to branch looking for food. Often a group will huddle together and rest with their heads between their legs.

Other Monkeys

The red uakari is very shy. He hides in the trees where no one can see him. If he is excited, his bald head goes an even brighter red.

Male mandrill monkeys have the most colourful faces of all furry animals. They also have bright red, purple and blue bottoms.

A male proboscis monkey has a very big nose — proboscis means nose. It gets even longer and droopier as the monkey grows older.

Where the Animals in this Book Live

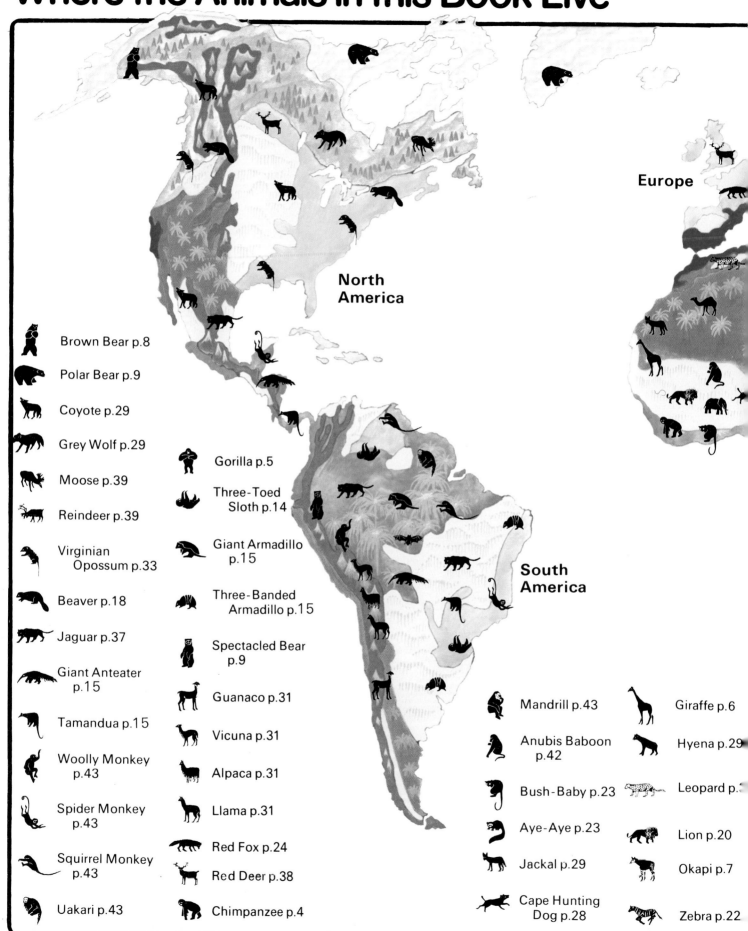

Europe

North America

South America

Brown Bear p.8

Polar Bear p.9

Coyote p.29

Grey Wolf p.29

Moose p.39

Reindeer p.39

Virginian Opossum p.33

Beaver p.18

Jaguar p.37

Giant Anteater p.15

Tamandua p.15

Woolly Monkey p.43

Spider Monkey p.43

Squirrel Monkey p.43

Uakari p.43

Gorilla p.5

Three-Toed Sloth p.14

Giant Armadillo p.15

Three-Banded Armadillo p.15

Spectacled Bear p.9

Guanaco p.31

Vicuna p.31

Alpaca p.31

Llama p.31

Red Fox p.24

Red Deer p.38

Chimpanzee p.4

Mandrill p.43

Anubis Baboon p.42

Bush-Baby p.23

Aye-Aye p.23

Jackal p.29

Cape Hunting Dog p.28

Giraffe p.6

Hyena p.29

Leopard p.

Lion p.20

Okapi p.7

Zebra p.22

Sloth Bear p.9

Giant Panda p.25

Tiger p.10

Chinese Water Deer p.39

Indian Elephant p.17

Bat p.34

Bactrian Camel p.30

Dingo p.29

Long-nosed Bandicoot p.33

Koala p.33

Red Kangaroo p.32

Asia

Africa

Australia

Rhino p.12

Hippo p.40

Cheetah p.37

African Elephant p.16

Arabian Camel p.30

Wildebeest p.26

Gibbon p.5

Siamang p.5

Proboscis Monkey p.43

Tarsier p.23

Slender Loris p.23

Sun Bear p.9

What the Colours Mean

Mountains		Warm Forests
Cold Forests		Hot, Wet Forests
Desert		Very Cold Lands
Grassy Plains		Scrub Land

Animal Facts and Figures

Animal	Average Size of Adult Male	Weight of Male	Carnivore	Herbivore	Gestation Period	Size of Litter	When the Animal Feeds	Climber	Life Span
Chimpanzee	1.5 m high	80 kg	Yes	Yes	7½ months	1 baby	Day	Yes	40 years
Gorilla	1.75 m high	275 kg	No	Yes	9 months	1 baby	Day	Yes	20–45 years
Giraffe	4 m high	1,800 kg	No	Yes	14–15 months	1–2 babies	Dawn/Dusk	No	15–20 years
Brown Bear	2.8 m long	780 kg	Yes	Yes	6–8 months	1–3 babies	Dusk/Night	Yes	30 years
Polar Bear	2.5 m long	410 kg	Yes	No	9 months	1–4 babies	Day	No	34 years
Tiger	2.8 m long	272 kg	Yes	No	3½ months	3–4 babies	Mainly Night	Yes	20 years
Black Rhino	3.75 m long	1,800 kg	No	Yes	17½–18 months	1 baby	Night/Dawn/Dusk	No	50 years
Three-toed Sloth	60 cm long	4.5 kg	No	Yes	4–6 months	1 baby	Night	Yes	under 12 years
Giant Anteater	1.2 m long	23 kg	Yes	No	6½ months	1 baby	Day or Night	No	14 years
Giant Armadillo	1 m long	50 kg	Yes	No	Not confirmed	1–2 babies	Night	No	15 years
Tamandua	58 cm long	5 kg	Yes	No	Not confirmed	1 baby	Night/Dawn/Dusk	Yes	10 years
African Elephant	3–4 m high	7,500 kg	No	Yes	22 months	1 baby	Day	No	50–70 years
Beaver	1.3 m long	32 kg	No	Yes	3–4 months	3–4 babies	Dusk	No	15–20 years
Lion	2.4 m long	227 kg	Yes	No	3½ months	2–5 babies	Night/Dawn/Dusk	Yes	20–25 years
Zebra	2.4 m long	350 kg	No	Yes	11½–13 months	1–2 babies	Mainly Night	No	28 years
Bushbaby (Senegal)	20 cm long	300 gms	Yes	Yes	4 months	1–3 babies	Night	Yes	10 years
Red Fox	1.4 m long	6 kg	Yes	Yes	1½–2 months	4–10 babies	Mainly Night	No	12 years
Giant Panda	1.3 m long	160 kg	Yes	Yes	7–9 months	1–2 babies	Day	Yes	15–30 years
Wildebeest	2 m long	275 kg	No	Yes	8–9 months	1 baby	Dawn/Dusk	No	16 years
Cape Hunting Dog	1 m long	27 kg	Yes	No	2½ months	6–8 babies	Night/Dawn/Dusk	No	10 years
Grey Wolf	1.3 m long	70 kg	Yes	No	2 months	5–7 babies	Day	No	14–16 years
Hyena	1.6 m long	82 kg	Yes	No	3½ months	1–2 babies	Night/Dawn/Dusk	No	25 years
Camel (Bactrian)	3 m long	690 kg	No	Yes	12½–14½ months	1–2 babies	Day/Dusk	No	45 years
Red Kangaroo	1.5 m long	70 kg	No	Yes	1 month	1 baby	Night	No	10–20 years
Koala	85 cm long	15 kg	No	Yes	1 month	1 baby	Night	Yes	20 years
Virginian Opossum	50 cm long	5.5 kg	Yes	Yes	13 days	8–18 babies	Night	Yes	2 years
Vampire Bat	9 cm long	50 gms	Yes	No	3–4 months	1 baby	Night	Yes	12 years
Leopard	1.5 m long	91 kg	Yes	No	3 months	2–3 babies	Night/Dawn/Dusk	Yes	15–20 years
Cheetah	1.5 m long	65 kg	Yes	No	3 months	2–4 babies	Day	Yes	15–30 years
Red Deer	2.5 m long	250 kg	No	Yes	8 months	1–2 babies	Dawn/Dusk	No	15–18 years
Moose	3 m long	825 kg	No	Yes	8 months	1–3 babies	Day	No	20 years
Hippo	4.6 m long	4,500 kg	No	Yes	7½–8 months	1–2 babies	Night	No	40–50 years
Baboon (Anubis)	1 m long	34 kg	Yes	Yes	6–7 months	1–2 babies	Dawn/Dusk	Yes	20 years
Spider Monkey	63 cm long	6 kg	Yes	Yes	4½ months	1 baby	Day	Yes	20 years
Woolly Monkey	68 cm long	6 kg	No	Yes	4½–5 months	1 baby	Day	Yes	20–25 years

46

Animal Words

Browser—an animal that feeds on the leaves and twigs of small bushes and trees.

Burrow—the den that some animals make to live in during the cold winter months or when they have their babies.

Carnivore—an animal that eats other animals, birds, fish or insects.

Chewing the cud—the food an animal brings back from its stomach into its mouth to chew again.

Gestation period—the length of time a female animal carries her babies inside her before they are born.

Harem—a group of female animals that have been chosen as mates by one male animal.

Herbivore—an animal that eats grass, leaves and plants but not meat.

Herd—a group of animals that feed or move together.

Hibernation—the time when some animals sleep or rest during the cold winter months.

Litter—a group of babies born at the same time to one mother.

Marsupial—a female animal that has a pouch for her baby to live and feed in until it is old enough to look after itself.

Migration—the yearly movements of herds of animals from one feeding ground to another and back again.

Nocturnal animal—an animal that rests or sleeps during the day and hunts and feeds at night.

Predator—an animal, like a lion, that hunts and kills other animals for food.

Prey—the animal that is killed by a predator.

Suckle—when a baby animal is fed by its mother on her milk.

Territory—the patch of land or water where an animal lives and feeds, and defends against other animals.

Index